Nimesh the Adventurer

Ranjit Singh   Mehrdokht Amini

Lantana

3001

...the
DRAGON!

Now we arrive at the bottom of the ocean.

FIRE EXIT

HAMMERHEAD
SHARK

Quiet Room

FIRST
AID

It looks like a
corridor to me,
Nimesh.

Corridor? Why
would a corridor
be full of...

...the North Pole!

Look at these glaciers of ice! Hear those avalanches of snow! Can you feel the ground tremble?

Watch as I skate across the ice
with my sleigh of dogs!

...a guardsman for the Indian Maharaja.

Oh really, Nimesh?

Oh yes, he told me so. He once backflipped right across the Maharaja's table...

...and didn't even smash or break anything!

...pirate ship!

Pirates don't scare me.
I'm Nimesh the
adventurer!

Royal Walk

We'll find a beach behind
those palm trees.

No, we'll find the local
park, Nimesh.

No,   we'll find...

And what's this, Nimesh?

Is it a cave full of gold?
Or an Emperor's castle?
Perhaps a lush forest?

This is
home.

For Mum, Dad, Bina and 'H'.
Ranjit

For Yara, Nora, Melody, Nona, Narvan, Borna, Misha
and all the little ones with big imaginations!
Mehrdokht

First published in the United Kingdom in 2018 by Lantana Publishing Ltd., Oxford, UK.
www.lantanapublishing.com | info@lantanapublishing.com

American edition published in 2018 by Lantana Publishing Ltd., UK.

Softcover edition published in 2019. Reprinted in 2022.

Distributed in the United States and Canada by Lerner Publishing Group, Inc.
241 First Avenue North, Minneapolis, MN 55401 U.S.A.
For reading levels and more information, look for this title at www.lernerbooks.com
Cataloging-in-Publication Data Available.

Printed and bound in Europe using sustainably sourced paper and plant-based inks.
Original artwork using mixed media, finished digitally.

Softcover ISBN: 978-1-911373-38-4
Hardcover ISBN: 978-1-911373-24-7
PDF ISBN: 978-1-911373-25-4
ePub3 ISBN: 978-1-911373-41-4